DAY BY DAY A WEEK GOES ROUND

by Carol Diggory Shields

illustrated by True Kelley

DUTTON CHILDREN'S BOOKS ✹ NEW YORK

FOR ZOOEY, WITH LOVE—C.D.S.
FOR ELOISE LINDBLOM—T.K.

✳

Text copyright © 1998 by Carol Diggory Shields
Illustrations copyright © 1998 by True Kelley

CIP Data is available.

Published in the United States 1998 by Dutton Children's Books.
a member of Penguin Putnam Inc.
375 Hudson Street. New York. New York 10014
Designed by Amy Berniker
Manufactured in China
First Edition
ISBN 0-525-45457-8
1 3 5 7 9 10 8 6 4 2

The sun comes up, the moon goes down,
By tick and tock a day goes round.
The days go dancing, one by one,
When seven pass, a week is done.
The moon is counting in the sky,
As week by week a month goes by.
Month by month the seasons swing,
Summer, autumn, winter, spring.
The moon comes up, the sun goes down,
And month by month a year goes round.

Monday, Monday,
rise and shine,
Everyone is hurrying
to be on time.

Zip, snap, button up,
don't be slow,

Monday, Monday,

ready, set, go!

Tuesday, Tuesday, groceries,
Milk, bread, crackers,
juice, and cheese.

Push-push, squeak-squeak
down the aisles,
Apples rise in shiny piles.

Pack it, bag it, time to pay,
Tuesday, Tuesday, shopping day.

Wednesday, Wednesday, Mother Goose,
Puppets, pop-ups, Dr. Seuss.

We hear stories, say a poem,
Make a project to take home.

Teddy bear, teddy bear, do you see me?

Wednesdays at the library.

Thursday, Thursday,
scrub-a-dub,

Wash and sweep and wipe and rub.

I can help, I clean my room,

Watch me push this great big broom!

See my toys
all in a line?

Thursday, Thursday, clean-up time.

Friday, Friday, with my friends,

Kenji,

Amber,

Joey,

Ben.

Hiding, sliding, all fall down,

Here's a bug
that Kenji found.

Count to ten and run away,
Friday, Friday, play-group day.

Saturday, Saturday,
digging down,
New green plants
go in the ground.

Wiggly worms in warm dark dirt,

Squiggly hose goes squirt, squirt, squirt.

Mix it, stir it, nice and muddly,
Saturday, Saturday, muddly-puddly.

Sunday, Sunday, snuggle bugs
Climb in bed for morning hugs.

Yawns and giggles, tickled tummies,
Momma reads the Sunday funnies.

Making pancakes, Dad and me,
Sunday, Sunday, family.

When the week is at an end,
Monday starts it up again.